January 23 is National Pie Day.

Mama’

Can you find these hidden pictures?

Illustrated by Charles Jordan

Picking Pumpkins

Fall begins on September 22, 2001.

crescent moon
fishhook
hammer
ice-cream cone
ladle
swan
canoe
hot dog
shoe
dog
teacup
sleigh
candle
Illustrated by Linda Weller

Soccer Practice

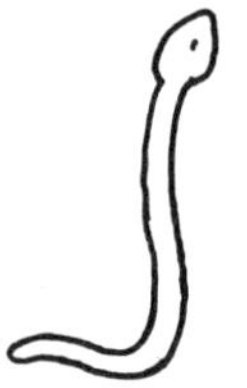

snake

artist's brush

bowl

drinking glass

flag

crayon

Can you find these hidden pictures?

mitten

radish

hammer

book

crown

spoon

Gator's Nap

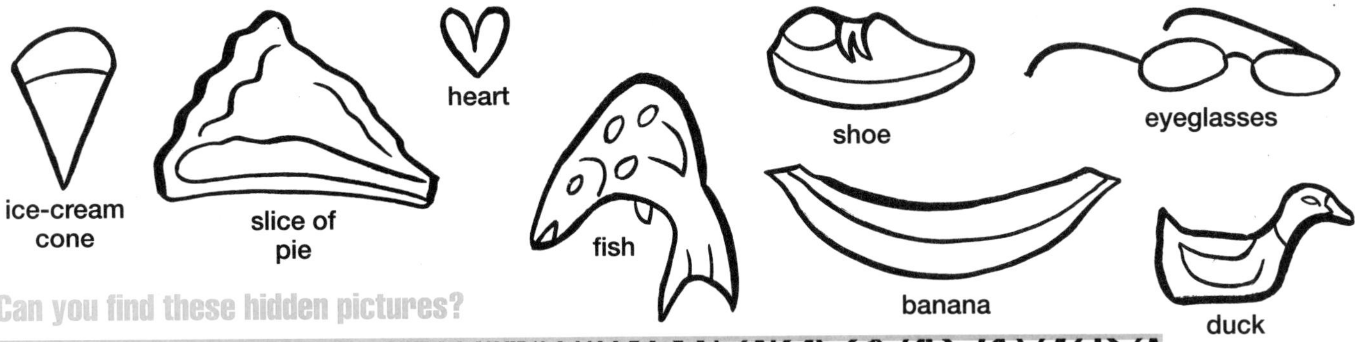

Can you find these hidden pictures?

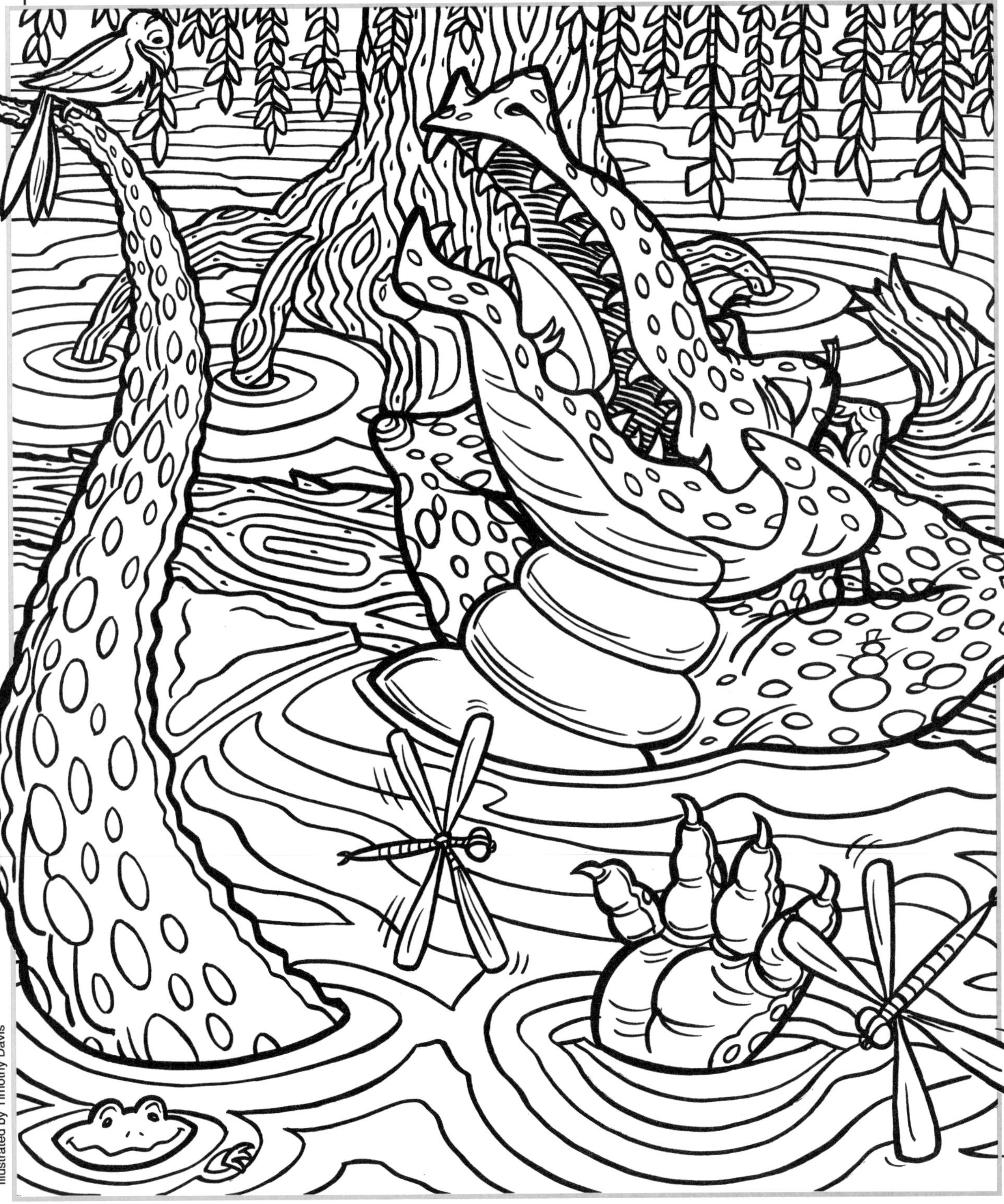

Illustrated by Timothy Davis

Two New Kittens

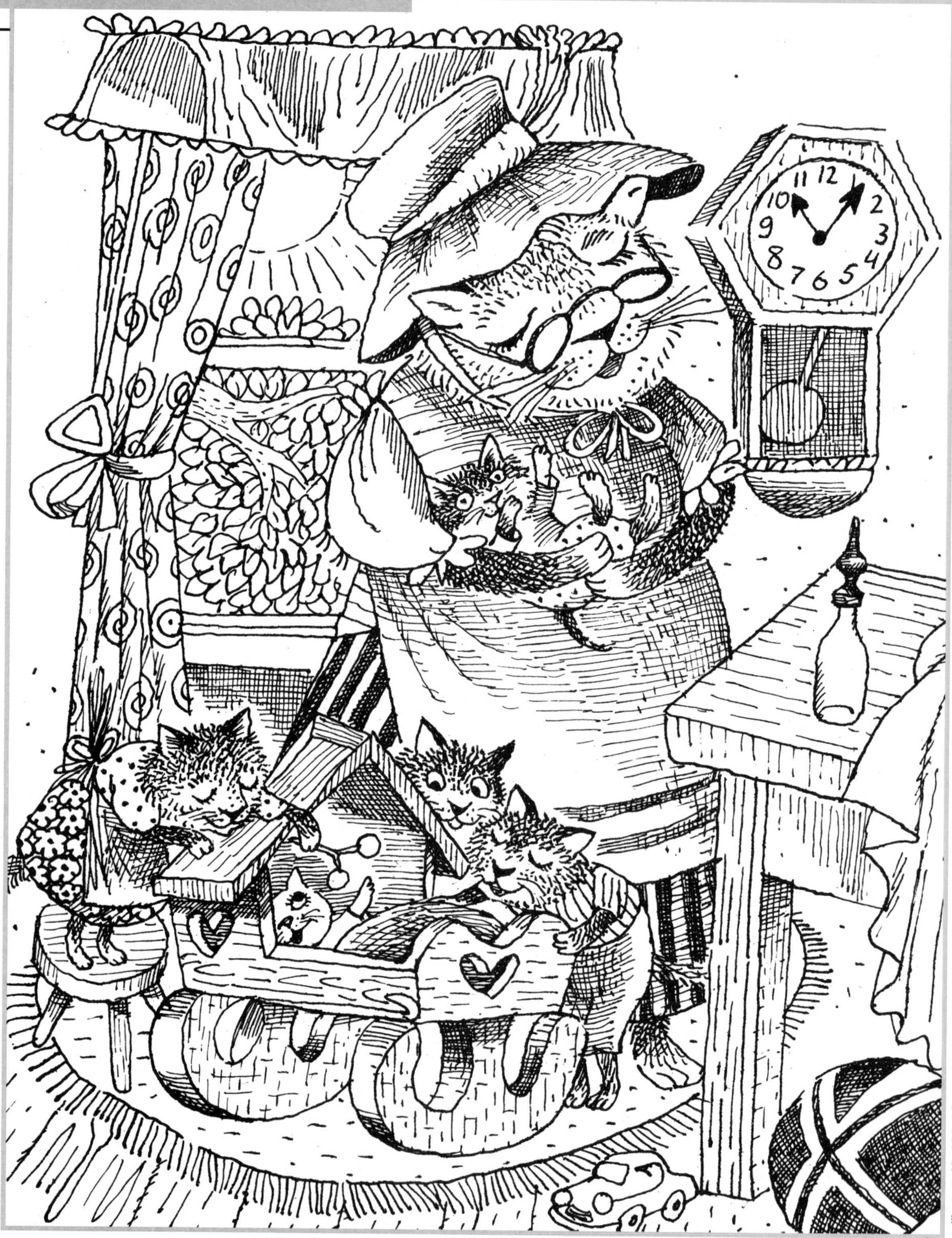

dustpan

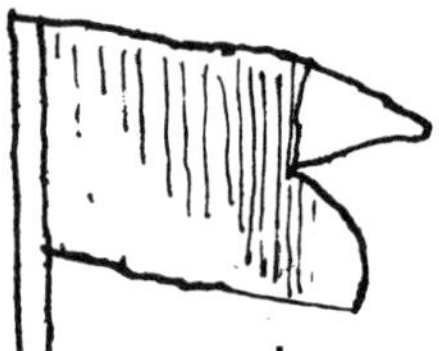
pennant

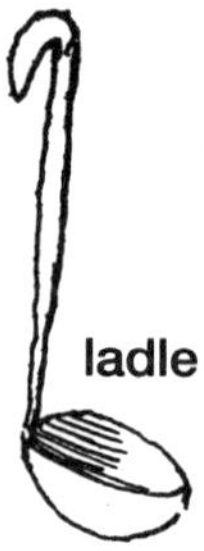
ladle

carrot

pencil

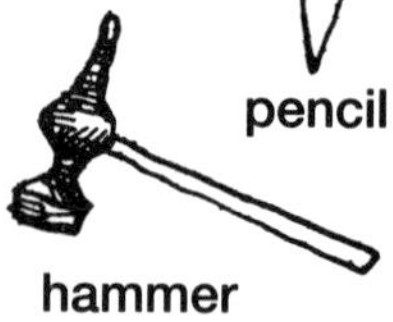
hammer

bird

turtle

Can you find these hidden pictures?

fishhook

chicken

fork

bouquet of flowers

key

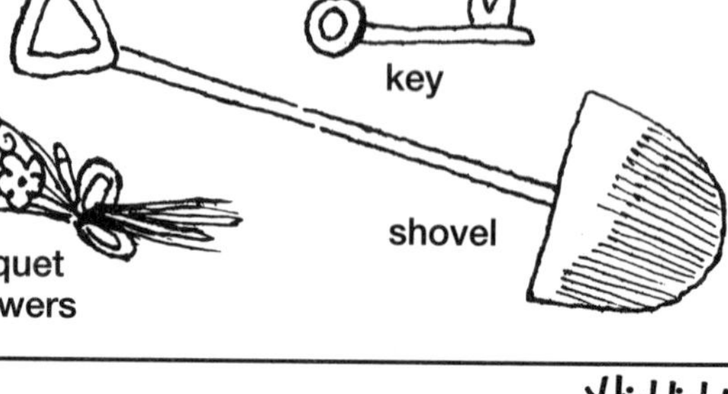
shovel

The first Nobel Prizes, founded by the Swiss inventor, were awarded in 1901—100 years ago.

Alfred Nobel

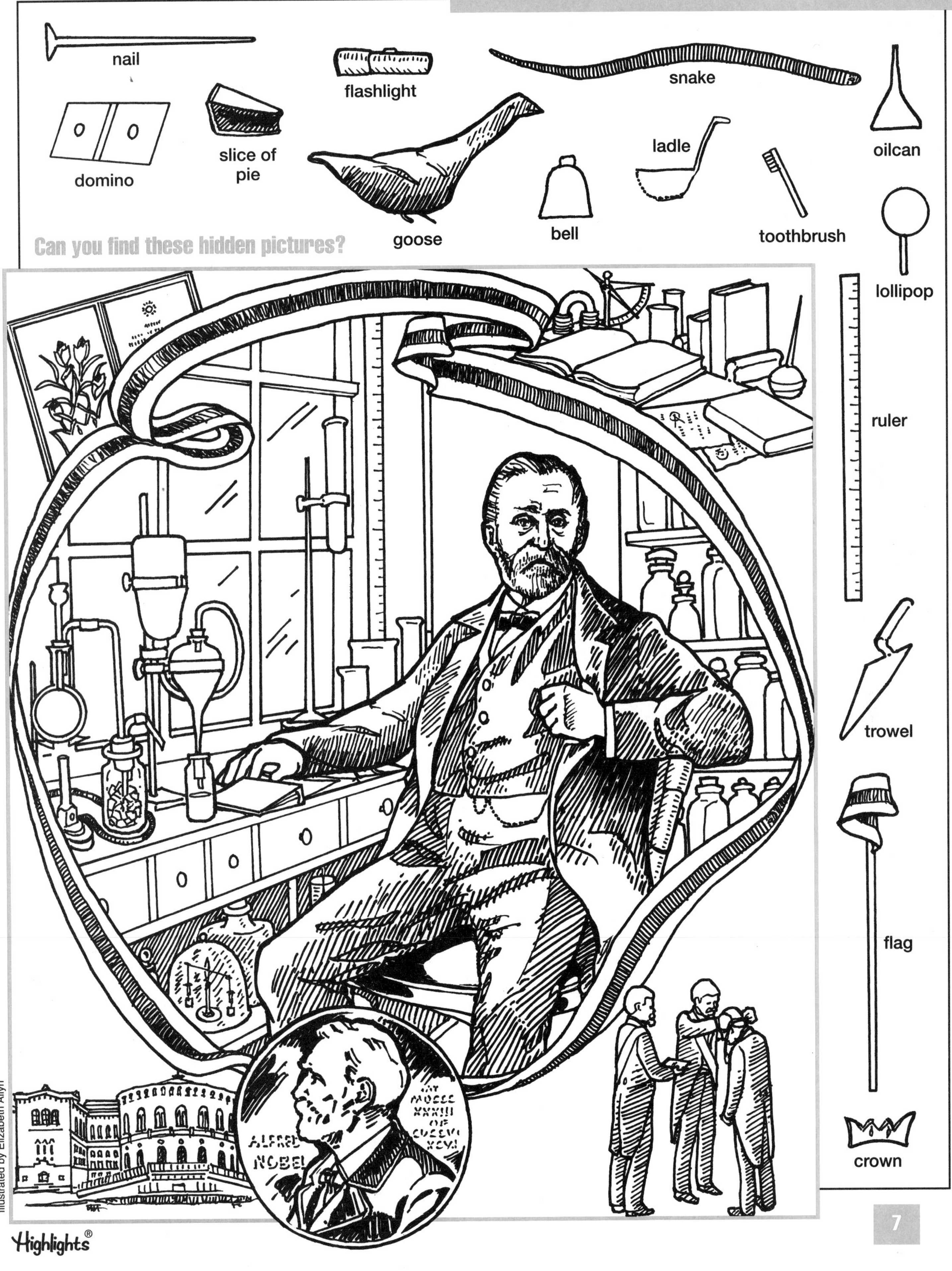

Illustrated by Elizabeth Allyn

Out-of-This-World Journey

July 15-21, 2001, is Space Week, marking the July 20, 1969, landing on the Moon.

Illustrated by Timothy Davis

teacup

saw

crown

bell

ice-cream cone

frog

candle

Can you find these hidden pictures?

banana

fish

light bulb

ring

sailboat

spoon

heart

toothbrush

Clean-up Crew

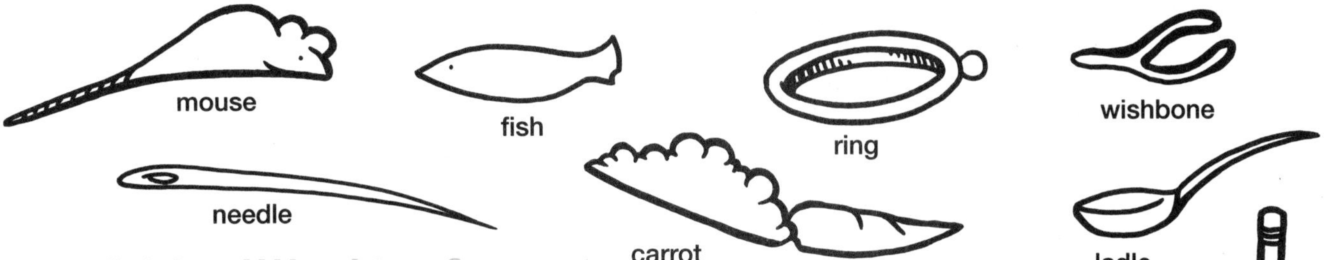

Can you find these hidden pictures?

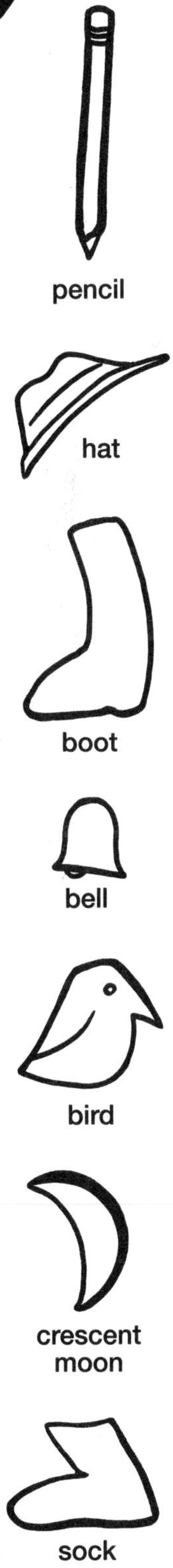

Ghostly Trick-or-treater

October 31 is National Magic Day.

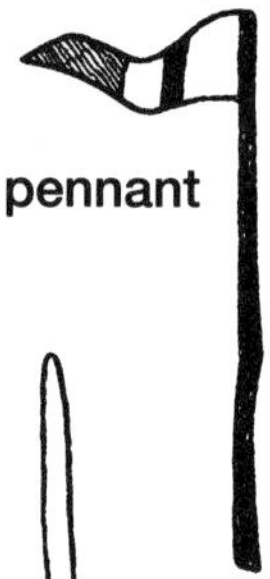
pennant

artist's brush

carrot

hammer

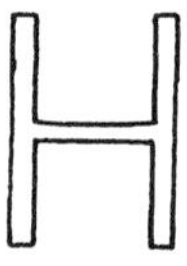
letter *H*

spatula

Can you find these hidden pictures?

fish

needle

spoon

book

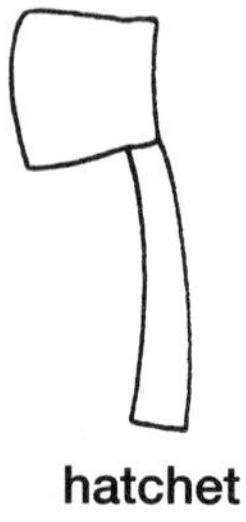
hatchet

tea bag

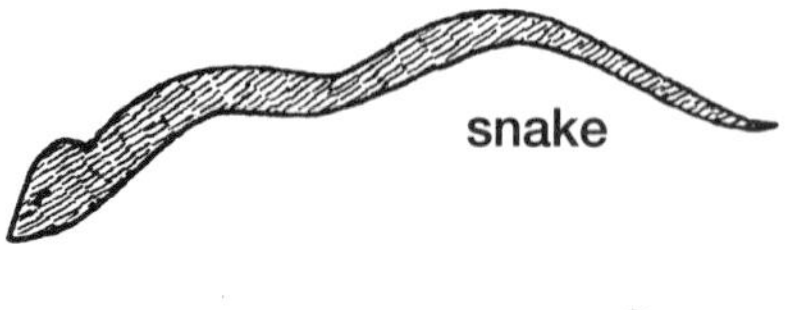
snake

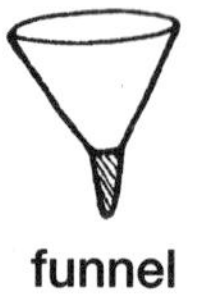
funnel

slice of pizza

Ride the Rapids

ice-cream cone
book
shark
bird
pencil
hanger
snake
mitten
Can you find these hidden pictures?
crescent moon
worm
ax
sailboat
teacup
hairbrush
WOWEE 200

Dinnertime Helpers

May 15 is International Day of Families.

telephone receiver

sailboat

toothbrush

bottle

carrot

Can you find these hidden pictures?

pear

golf club

boot

light bulb

in-line skate

banana

ring

baseball bat
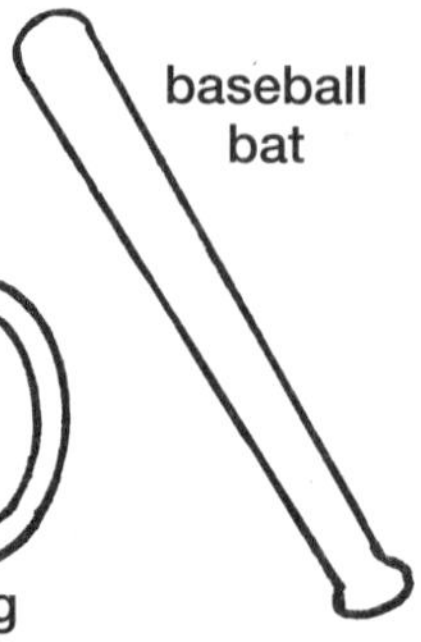

pencil

Winter begins on December 21, 2001.

Snow-Loving Bears

muffin

ice-cream sundae

sneaker

carrot

heart

ice-cream pop

sheep

banana

Can you find these hidden pictures?

dog

caramel apple

duck

paintbrush

snake

Robot Restaurant

ice-cream pop

hatchet

bolt

donut

diamond

pail

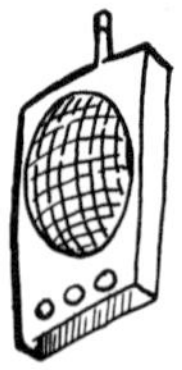

radio

Can you find these hidden pictures?

worm

ring

telescope

lamp

light bulb

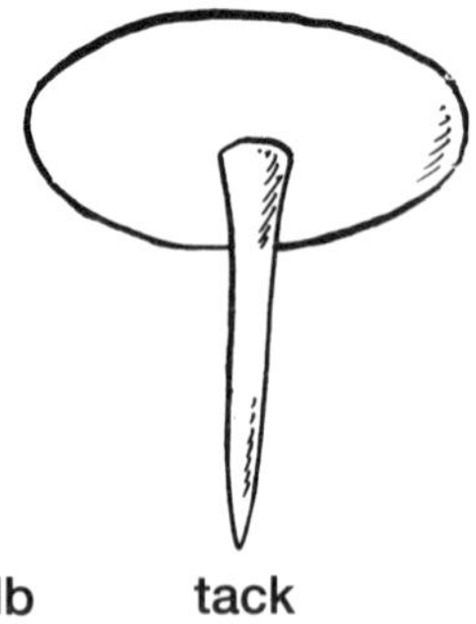

tack

Fun on Wheels

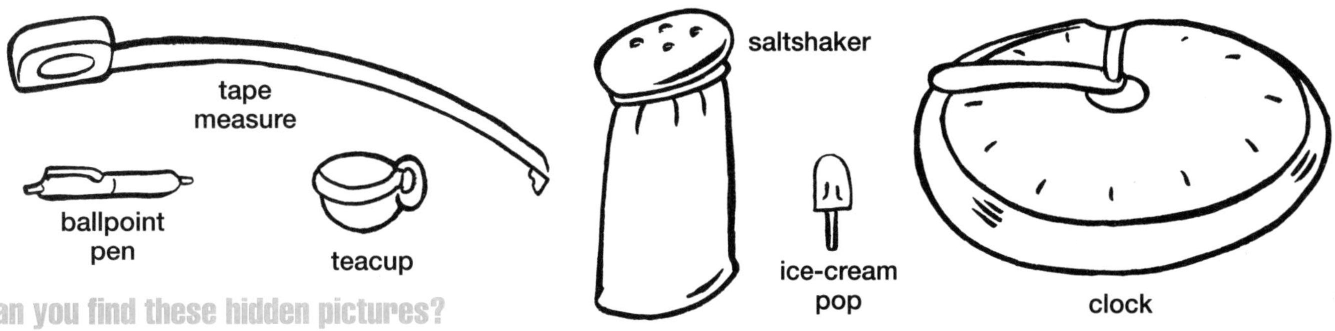

Can you find these hidden pictures?

Library Pals

National Library Week is April 1-7, 2001.

potholder

spatula

pencil

golf club

candle

Can you find these hidden pictures?

dustpan

flashlight

celery

crayon

leaf

bell

slice of bread

Motorized Marvel

One hundred years ago, engines were added to bicycles to create one of the first motorcycles.

Can you find these hidden pictures?

Illustrated by Elizabeth Allyn

Bedtime Story

January is National Book Month.

Illustrated by Maurie Jo Manning

mitten

sailboat

baseball

apple core

spoon

crescent moon

Can you find these hidden pictures?

clothespin

banana

raindrop

toothbrush

feather

paintbrush

February 11-18, 2001, is Homes for Birds Week.

Birdbath Buddies

hammer

sock

slice of pie

heart

glove

paper clip

shark

snail

star

crescent moon

sailboat

toothbrush

pencil

banana

Can you find these hidden pictures?

Fishing by Moonlight

slipper

toothbrush

sailboat

cat

paper clip

ice-cream cone

pliers

boot

Can you find these hidden pictures?

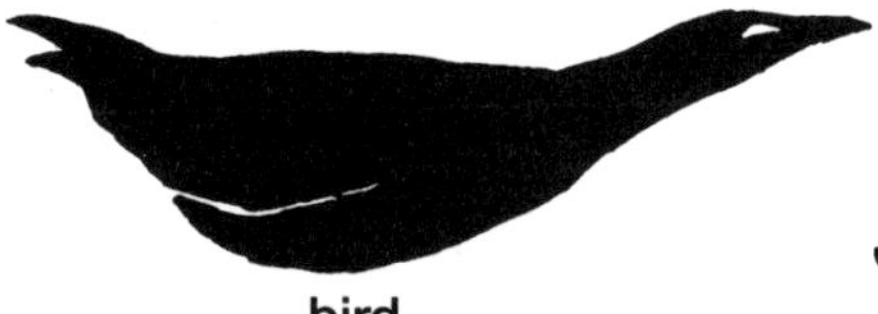
bird

crescent moon

bat

hat

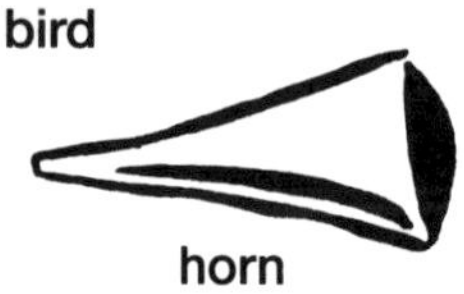
horn

mitten

banana

artist's brush
tweezers
bottle
spoon
goose
feather
dinosaur
duck
carrot
fork
lobster
Illustrated by Timothy Davis

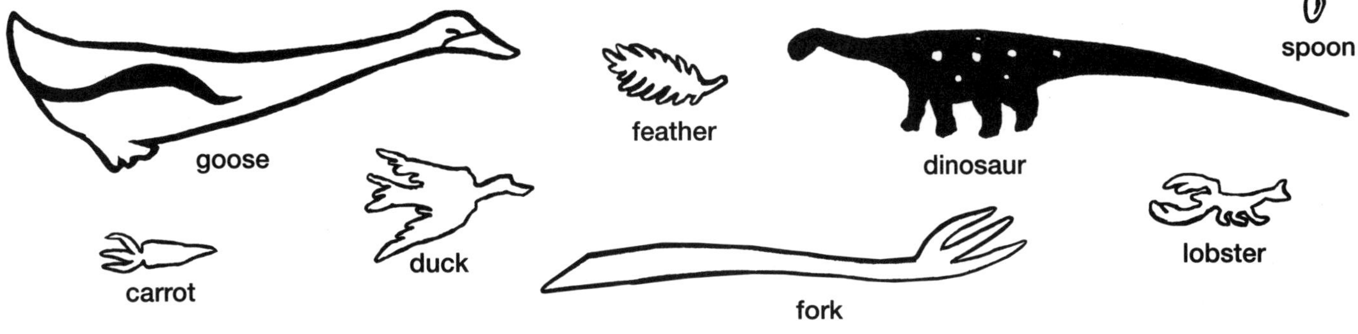

Spring Planting

National Garden Week is April 8-14, 2001.

Illustrated by R. Michael Palan

cap

teacup

hammer

candle

wristwatch

drumstick

candy cane

pennant

Can you find these hidden pictures?

golf club

spoon

book

needle

toothbrush

banana

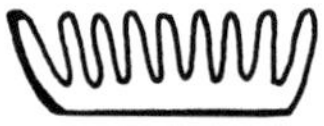
comb

rabbit

tube of toothpaste

April 23-29, 2001, is Reading Is Fun Week.

Story Hour at the Library

cap

high-heeled shoe

goose

bowling pin

slipper

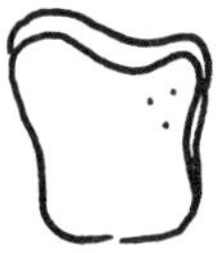
slice of bread

Can you find these hidden pictures?

watering can

bell

pear

feather

worm

slice of apple

Highlights®

Stunt Driver

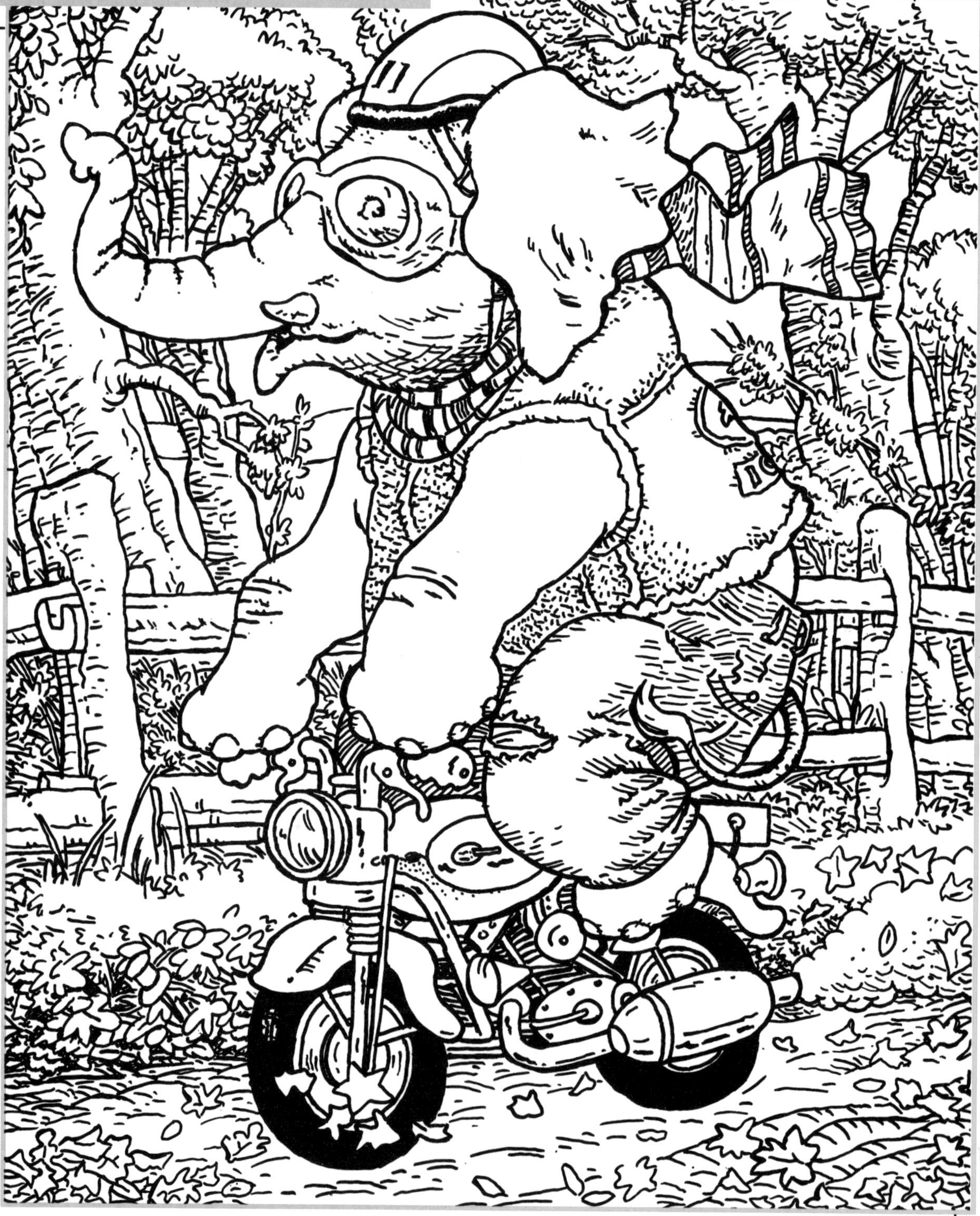

teacup

ballpoint pen

oilcan

slice of cake

magnifying glass

carrot

Can you find these hidden pictures?

ice-cream cone

book

pencil

wrench

pushpin

paintbrush

bell

October is National Pizza Month.

Pizza Party

Illustrated by Larry Daste

Art Show

March is Youth Art Month.

Welcome to Our Art Show
My dinosaur is glad
by Dani
in Winter I feed the birds.
by Robin
I love to dan
The
I am the Queen.
My dog is nice
by JOEY

Illustrated by Maurie Jo Manning

saltshaker

high-heeled shoe

magnet

lollipop

crayon

goose

tack

Can you find these hidden pictures?

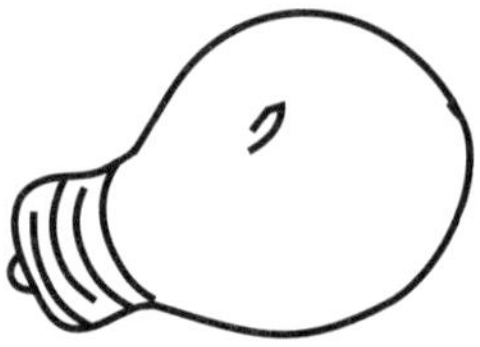
light bulb

bird

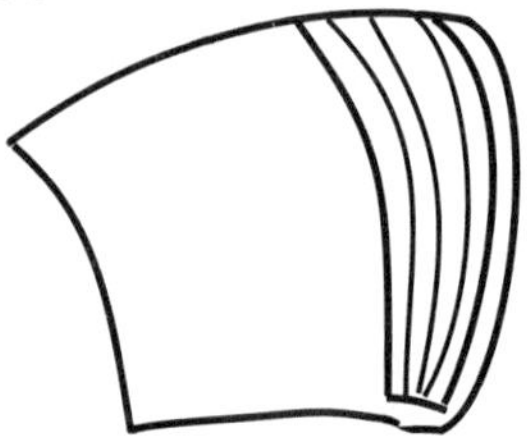
book

mitten

paintbrush

Bookworms

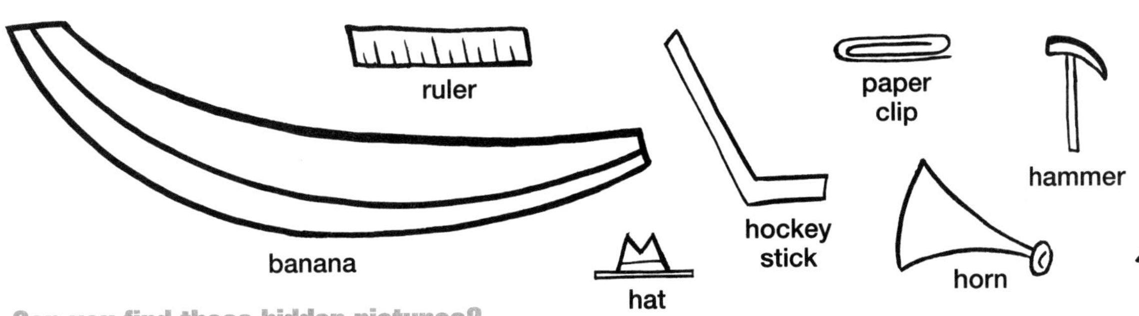

Can you find these hidden pictures?

Illustrated by Timothy Davis

Animals on Ice

bird

mouse

dragonfly

in-line skate

hairbrush

Can you find these hidden pictures?

squirrel

iron

hammer

fork

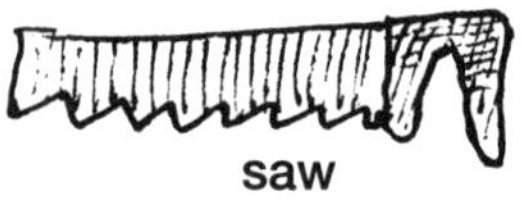

saw

turtle

Illustrated by Valeri Gorbachev

shoe

penguin

arrow

vase

hanger

pennant

teapot

fishhook

spoon

strawberry

key

dustpan

Odorous Guests

toothbrush

egg

book

handbell

comb

Illustrated by Timothy Davis

Can you find these hidden pictures?

bat

heart

2 chickens

banana

crown

sneaker

fish

mitten

Grandparents' Day is on September 9, 2001.

Grandma Sets the Pace

spoon

lollipop

clothespin

banana

high-heeled shoe

bell

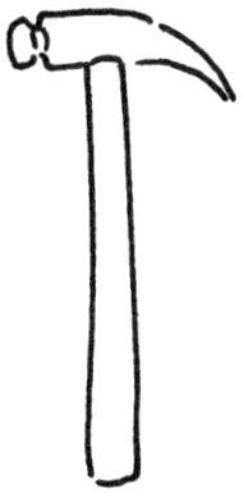
hammer

fork

Can you find these hidden pictures?

sheep

feather

teacup

bird

hatchet

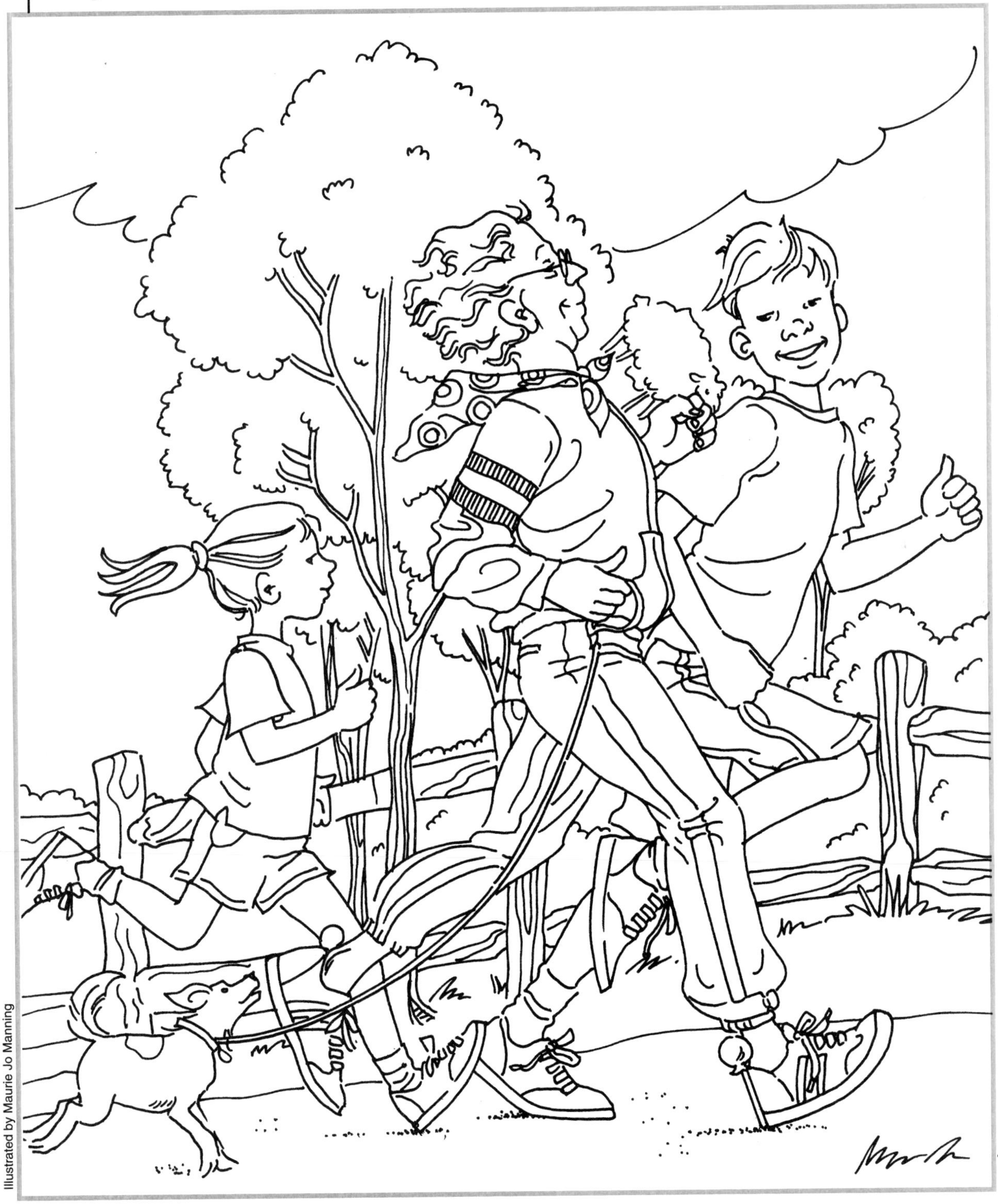

Illustrated by Maurie Jo Manning

On the Balance Beam

Illustrated by Janet Robertson

Can you find these hidden pictures?

nail

paper bag

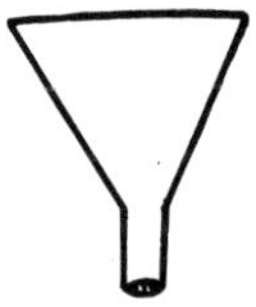
funnel

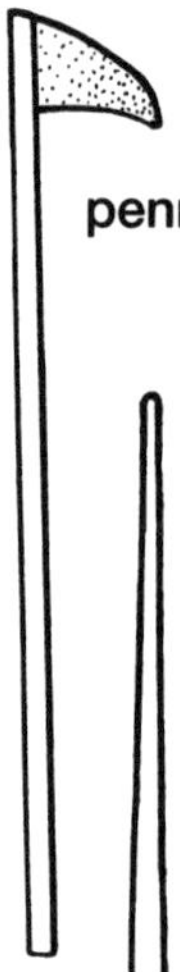
pennant

artist's brush

mug

candle

fishhook

top hat

needle

tube of toothpaste

toothbrush

mushroom

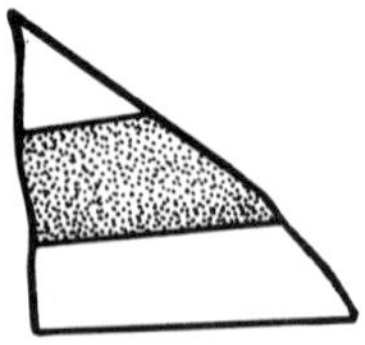
party hat

slice of pie

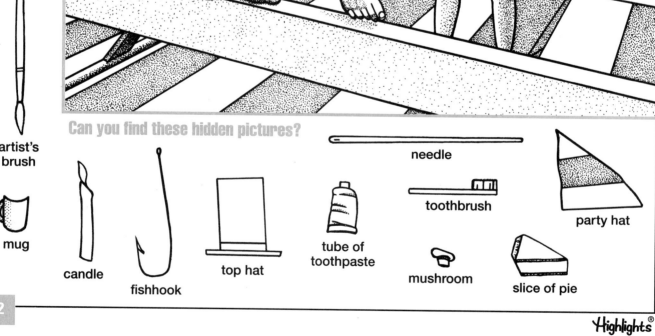

Our third President was the first to be inaugurated in Washington, D.C., in 1801—200 years ago.

Jefferson's Inauguration

loaf of bread

fish

slice of lemon

pail

crescent moon

pennant

hammer

toothbrush

Can you find these hidden pictures?

bowling pin

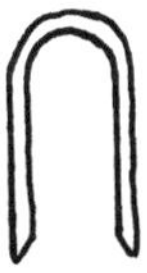
staple

ladder

carrot

bird

Aardvark Artist

candle

tack

slice of cake

whistle

spoon

Can you find these hidden pictures?

saucepan

wishbone

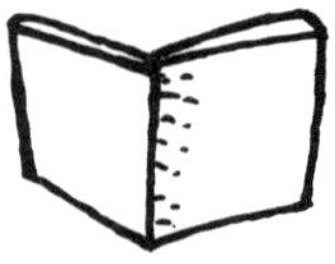
open book

candy

dog bone

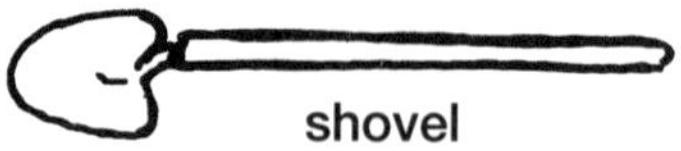
shovel

ring

October 7-13, 2001, is Fire Prevention Week.

Safety Lesson

Family Picnic

Can you find these hidden pictures?

T-shirt

ice-cream cone

comb

toothbrush

glove

artist's brush

hat

saw

heart

crown

crescent moon

bell

bat

fish

Beavers at Work

Can you find these hidden pictures?

goose
toothbrush
banana
fish
glove
slice of pie
bird
comb
saw
pencil
lizard
crown
candle
paper clip
open book
carrot
tweezers

Catch of the Day

hat

carrot

wishbone

snake

ring

nail

crescent moon

Can you find these hidden pictures?

needle

heart

apple

fishhook

golf club

artist's brush

crayon

slipper

Page 1

Pages 2-3

Answers

▼Page 4

▼Page 5

▼Page 6

▼Page 7

Page 8

Page 9

Page 10

Page 11

Answers

Page 12

Page 13

Page 14

Page 15

Page 16

Page 17

Page 18

Page 19

Pages 20-21

Page 22

Page 23

Page 24

Page 25

AL'S PIZZA WELCOMES THE TIGERS !!...
CELEBRATING A SEASON OF SPORTSMANSHIP
AL'S PIZZAS

Page 26

Welcome to Our Art Show
My dinosaur is glad
by Dani
in Winter I feed the birds.
by Robin
I am the Queen.
My dog is nice
by JOEY

Page 27

READING
AROUND the WORLD in 80 DAYS

Answers

Pages 28-29

Page 30

Page 31

Page 32

Page 33

Page 34

Page 35

Answers

Page 36

Page 37

Page 38

Cover